SHERLOCK HOLMES

THE SUSSEX VAMPIRE

SIR ARTHUR CONAN DOYLE

Sweet Cherry
PUBLISHING

SHERLOCK HOLMES

THE
SUSSEX
VAMPIRE

SIR ARTHUR CONAN DOYLE

By the autumn of 1901, my
medical practice was well
established and kept me very
busy. This had an unfortunate
effect on my friendships and I
found myself feeling rather cut
off from the world.

I had not seen my friend
Sherlock Holmes for a
particularly long time, so I
decided to pay him a call one

November afternoon. I rang the bell at 221B Baker Street and I was greeted by Mrs Hudson, who gave me a beaming smile. Perhaps she had missed me. I doubted that Holmes had been very good company, especially if he had been busy with cases.

As I climbed the stairs to our old sitting room I wondered whether things had changed since I last saw him. It was a comfort to find that instead we immediately fell back into our old routine. Indeed it was only a few minutes before I was reading my newspaper in front of the blazing fire while sipping at the coffee Mrs Hudson had kindly brought up.

Meanwhile, Holmes had been carefully reading a note that the last post had brought him. Then, with a dry chuckle that was his nearest approach to a laugh, he tossed it over to me. 'For a mixture of modern and medieval, this is surely the limit. What do you think of it, Watson?'

I put aside my newspaper, took up the letter, and began to read.

46 Old Jewry
November 19th

Re: Vampires
Sir — Our client, Mr Robert Ferguson, of Ferguson and Muirhead, tea brokers, Mincing Lane, London, has made an enquiry from us concerning vampires. As our firm specialises entirely in the assessment of machinery, the matter is not one upon which we can advise. We have therefore recommended that Mr Ferguson call upon you. We have not forgotten your successful action in the case of Matilda Briggs.

We are, sir, faithfully yours,
Morrison, Morrison and Dodd

I read the last line carefully. Furrowing my brow, I tried to remember if Holmes had ever introduced me to this client, but drew a blank. When I looked up, I caught an amused expression on Holmes' face before it changed to that familiar faraway look as the detective reached back into his memory. 'Matilda Briggs was not the name of a young woman, Watson,' said Holmes. 'It was a ship that is associated with the giant rat of Sumatra, a story for which the world is not yet prepared.'

I raised an eyebrow, half expecting an explanation, but none came. Instead I made a mental note to enquire about this giant rodent another time and kept silent. Holmes hated to be sidetracked.

'But what do we know about vampires?' went on Holmes. 'Does it come within our expertise? Anything is better than doing nothing, but really, we seem to have stumbled into a Grimm's fairy tale. Stretch out your arm, Watson, and see what is in the book under V.'

I leaned back, took down the great index volume, and handed it to him. Holmes balanced it on his knee and his eyes moved slowly and lovingly over the record of old cases, mixed with information gathered over a lifetime.

'Voyage of the *Gloria Scott*,'

he read. 'That was a bad business. I remember that you made a record of it, Watson. Though I was unable to congratulate you on the result.' He looked up at me briefly, a twinkle in his eye. Being a man who dealt only with hard facts, he disliked the way I reported our cases and often teased me about it. Determined not to react, I instead kept my face expressionless and waited patiently for him to return his attention to the book still perched in his lap.

Holmes clearly realised that he was not going to get a rise out of me and looked slightly disappointed. Focussing once more on the book he continued. 'Victor Lynch, forger. Venomous lizard, or gila.

Remarkable case, that. Vittoria,
the circus belle. Vipers. Vogir,
the Hammersmith wonder.
Good old index! You can't
beat it. Listen to this, Watson.
Vampirism in Hungary.
And again, vampires in
Transylvania.'

He turned over the pages
with eagerness and briefly
fell silent, but after a short,
intense read, he threw down
the great book with a snarl of
disappointment.

'Rubbish, Watson, rubbish! What have we to do with walking corpses who can only be held in their graves by a stake driven through their hearts? It's pure lunacy.'

'But surely,' I said, 'the vampire was not necessarily a dead man. A living person could show such behaviour.

I have heard of the custom of older people sucking the blood from the young in order to retain their youth.'

'You are right, Watson. It mentions the legend in one of these references. But are we to give serious attention to such things? Our investigations have always been based firmly on fact, and there they must remain. No ghosts need apply. I do not think we can take Mr Robert Ferguson very seriously.'

He picked
up a second letter
that had lain unnoticed
on the table while he had
been absorbed with the first.
'Possibly this note may be from
him, and may throw some light
upon what is worrying him.'

He began to read it with a
smile of amusement on his face,
but it gradually faded away
into an expression of intense
interest and concentration.
When he had finished he sat

for some time lost in thought, with the letter dangling from his fingers. Finally, he roused himself from his daydream.

'Cheeseman's, Lamberley. Where is Lamberley, Watson?'

'It is in Sussex, south of Horsham.'

'Not very far, eh? And Cheeseman's?'

'I know that country, Holmes. It's full of old houses that are named after the men who built them centuries ago.

You get Odley's and Harvey's and Carriton's – the folk are forgotten but their names live on in their houses.'

'Precisely,' said Holmes coldly. I was a little taken aback by his sudden change of mood. Was he irritated at my knowledge, or that men should crave immortality in their house names? Holmes was so used to patiently explaining such things to me that perhaps I had reminded him that even he did not know everything. Regardless, I could see that he had added this new morsel to the vast amount of knowledge already contained within his mind. He absorbed new information quickly and accurately, but he rarely acknowledged the source of that information. I expected no credit.

'I rather think we shall know a lot more about Cheeseman's, Lamberley, before we are through. As I had hoped, the letter is from Robert Ferguson. By the way, he says that he knows you.'

'Knows me!'

'You had better read it.' He handed me the letter.

Dear Mr Holmes,

I have been recommended to you by my lawyers, but the matter is so extraordinarily delicate that it is most difficult to discuss. It concerns a friend for whom I am acting.

About five years ago this gentleman married a Peruvian lady. She was very beautiful, but they had no interests in common. After a time, his love towards his bride faded

and he worried that the
marriage had been a mistake.
He felt that there were
sides of her character that
he could never understand.
This was all the more
painful because she was a
loving wife, and absolutely
devoted to him.

Now for the mystery
at the heart of this story.
I will give you more detail
when we meet; this letter

is intended to give you a general idea of the strange situation. I hope that it will help you to decide whether you will investigate this matter.

The lady began to behave quite unlike her normal sweet and gentle nature. The gentleman had been married twice and had a son by the first wife. The boy is now

fifteen, a very charming and
affectionate youth, although
unfortunately injured in a
childhood accident. Twice the
wife was caught in the act of
assaulting this poor lad for
no apparent reason. Once
she struck him with a stick and
left a great mark on his arm.
But this was a small matter
compared with her conduct
to her own child, a dear boy

just under a year old. About a month ago the child was left by his nurse for a few minutes but she ran back when she heard him cry out loudly, as if in pain. As she ran into the room she saw the lady leaning over the baby and apparently biting his neck. There was a small wound in his neck, from which came a stream of blood.

Since beginning my association with Holmes, I had witnessed all sorts of bizarre and disturbing behaviour, but this letter described such horrors that I found myself having to pause for a moment. I wondered if Holmes had felt the same, but his face was now unreadable.

The nurse was so horrified that she went to call the husband, but the lady begged her not to do so, and actually gave her five pounds as a price for her silence. No explanation was ever given.

It left a terrible impression on the nurse's mind, and from that time she began to watch her employer closely, and to keep a closer guard over the baby. It seemed to her that the mother was also watching her, and that every time she was forced to leave the baby alone, the mother was waiting to get at him. Day and night the nurse stayed with the baby, and all the while the silent, watchful mother seemed to be lying in wait like a wolf waits for a lamb.

This must seem unbelievable, and yet I beg you to take it seriously, for a child's life and a man's sanity may depend upon it.

At last there came one dreadful day when the nurse could bear it no longer. She told the husband everything.

To him it seemed as wild a tale as it must seem to you now. He knew that his wife was a loving woman, despite her dislike of her step-son. Why then should she hurt her dear little baby? He told the nurse that her suspicions were mad and that he would not tolerate such things being said about his wife. While they were talking, however, there was a sudden cry of pain, and they both rushed to the nursery.

Imagine his feelings, Mr Holmes, when he saw his wife kneeling beside the cot, and blood on the child's neck. With a cry of horror, he turned his wife's face to the light and saw blood all round her lips. It was she — beyond question — who had drunk the poor baby's blood.

She is now confined to her room. There has been no explanation. The husband is half demented. He knows, and I know, very little about vampirism. We had thought it was some wild tale from foreign parts, and yet here it is in the very heart of Sussex

Will you see me? Will you use your great powers in aiding a man at his wits' end?

If so, kindly send a telegram to Ferguson, Cheeseman's, Lamberley, and I will be at your rooms at ten o'clock.

Yours faithfully,

Robert Ferguson

P.S. I believe your friend Watson played rugby for Blackheath when I was a three-quarter for Richmond.

'Of course I remember him,' I said, as I laid down the letter. 'Big Bob Ferguson, the finest three-quarter Richmond ever had. He was always a good-natured chap. It's just like him to be so concerned over a friend's case.'

Holmes looked at me thoughtfully and shook his head. 'Rugby, eh? I just don't know you, Watson. There are unexplored possibilities about you. Take a telegram down, like a good fellow.'

I picked up a pen
and paper ready.

'*Will examine your case
with pleasure,*' he dictated.

I looked up. '*Your* case!'

'We must not let him think
we are weak-minded. Of course
it is his case. Send him that
telegram and let the matter rest
until morning.'

I gave the matter a lot
of thought as I walked to
the telegraph office. Like

Holmes, I did not believe in the supernatural, but I could not think what could possibly explain such a bizarre chain of events. I looked forward to the following day, when Ferguson could provide us with some answers.

Promptly at ten o'clock the next morning, Ferguson strode into our room. I had remembered him as a tall man with loose limbs who was very fast on his feet, which had given him great success on the rugby field. There is surely nothing in life more painful than to meet the wreck of a fine athlete whom one has known in his prime. His great frame had fallen in, his blond hair was thin, and his shoulders were bowed. I feared that he would think similarly of me.

'Hello, Watson,' he said warmly, and his voice was still deep and hearty. 'You don't look quite the man you did when I threw you over the ropes into the crowd at Old Deer Park. I expect I have changed a bit also. But it is this last day or two that has aged me. I see by your telegram, Mr Holmes, that it is no use pretending to be anyone's deputy. I am the subject of the case.'

'It is simpler to deal direct,' said Holmes.

'Of course it is. But you can imagine how difficult it is when you are speaking of the woman you are bound to protect and help. What can I do? How am I to go to the police with such a story? And yet the children must be protected. Is it madness, Mr Holmes? Is it something in the blood? Have you any similar case in your experience? For heaven's sake give me some advice, for I am at my wits' end.'

'Very naturally, Mr Ferguson. Now sit here and pull yourself together, and give me a few clear answers. I can assure you that I am very far from being at my wits' end, and that I am confident we shall find some solution. First of all, tell me what you have done so far. Is your wife still near the children?'

'We had a dreadful scene. My wife is a most loving woman, Mr Holmes. If ever a woman loved a man with all her heart and soul, she loves me. She was devastated that I should have discovered this horrible secret. She would not even speak. She gave no answer to my accusations except to gaze at me with a sort of wild, despairing look in her eyes. Then she rushed to her room and locked herself in.

Since then she has refused to see me. She has a maid who was with her before our marriage, Dolores by name – a friend rather than an employee, and the only one allowed to see her. She takes her food to her.'

'Then the child is in no immediate danger?'

'Mrs Mason, the nurse, has sworn that she will not leave him, day or night. I can absolutely trust her. I am more

worried about poor little Jack,
for as I told you in my note, he
has twice been assaulted by
my wife.'

'But never wounded?'

'Not to my knowledge, but
she struck him savagely. It is
the all more terrible because he
is disabled.' Ferguson's weary
features softened as he spoke
of his boy. 'You would think
that the dear lad's condition
would soften anyone's heart.
A fall in childhood and a

twisted spine, Mr Holmes. But the dearest, most loving heart within.'

Holmes had picked up yesterday's letter and was reading it over. 'What other residents are there in your house, Mr Ferguson?'

'Two house staff who have not been long with us. One stable-hand, Michael, who sleeps in the house. My wife, myself, my boy Jack, the baby, Dolores, and Mrs Mason. That is all.'

'I gather that you did not know your wife well at the time of your marriage?'

'I had only known her a few weeks.'

'How long had this maid Dolores been with her?'

'Some years.'

'Then she would know your wife's character better than you do?'

'Yes, you may say so.'

Holmes made a note.

'I think,' he said, 'that I may be of more use at Lamberley than here. It is definitely a case for personal investigation. If the lady stays in her room, our presence would not annoy or inconvenience her. Of course, we would stay at the inn.'

Ferguson gave a gesture of relief.

'That is what I'd hoped, Mr Holmes. There is an excellent train at two from Victoria, if you could come.'

'Of course we shall come. There is a lull in cases at present. I can give you my undivided energies. Watson, of course, comes with us.'

Although I enjoyed working alongside Holmes on his cases, there was a part of

me that was irritated by his
assumption that I could ignore
my patients and my own work
to do so. At least the practice
was quiet, so my absence
would not cause a problem.

If my irritation showed on
my face, Holmes, of course,
either did not notice or chose to
ignore it. Instead he continued
to talk to Ferguson.

'But there are one or two
points upon which I wish to
be very sure before I begin my

investigations. This unhappy lady, I understand, has appeared to assault both the children: her own baby and your little son?'

'That is so.'

'But the results take different forms, do they not? She has beaten your son.'

'Yes. Once with a stick and once very savagely with her hands.'

'Did she give no explanation as to why she struck him?'

'None, except that she hated him. Again and again she said so.'

'Is the lady jealous by nature?'

'Yes, she is very jealous – with all the strength of her fiery love.'

'But the boy – he is fifteen, I understand, and although disabled physically, he is sound in mind? Did he give you any explanation of these assaults?'

'No. He declared there was no reason.'

'Were they good friends at other times?'

'No. There was never any love between them.'

'Yet you say he is affectionate?'

'Never in the world could there be a son so devoted. My life is his life.'

Once again Holmes made a note. For some time he sat lost in thought.

'No doubt you and the boy were great friends before this second marriage. You and he were close?'

'Very much so.'

'And the boy was very devoted to the memory of his mother?'

'Most devoted.'

'He would certainly seem to be a most interesting lad. There is one other point about these assaults. Were the strange attacks on the baby and the assaults upon your son during the same time period?'

'In the first case it was so. It was as if some frenzy had seized her and she had vented her rage upon both. In the second case it was only Jack who suffered. Mrs Mason had no complaint to make about the baby.'

'That certainly complicates matters.'

'I don't quite follow you, Mr Holmes.'

'Possibly not. One forms certain theories in the beginning and waits for more knowledge to confirm or dismiss them. A bad habit, Mr Ferguson, but human nature is weak. I fear that my old friend Watson here has given an exaggerated view of my scientific methods. However, I will only say at the present moment that your problem does not appear to me to be unsolvable, and that you may expect to find us at Victoria Station at two o'clock.'

It was a dull, foggy November day and we did indeed catch the two o'clock train to Lamberley. Then, having left our bags at the Chequers, we drove through a long, winding lane of Sussex clay to the isolated and ancient farmhouse

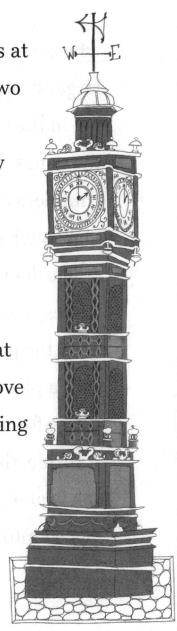

57

where Ferguson lived. It was a large, straggling building, very old in the centre, very new in the wings, with towering Tudor chimneys and a lichen-spotted, high-pitched roof.

The doorsteps were worn into curves, and the ancient tiles that lined the porch were engraved with a picture of a cheese and a man, after the original builder.

Inside, the ceilings bore heavy oak beams, and the uneven floor sagged into sharp curves. An odour of age and decay filled the whole crumbling building.

There was one very large central room, into which Ferguson led us. There was a huge old-fashioned fireplace with an iron screen behind it, and in the grate there blazed a splendid log fire.

As we took our seats in front of the fire, I gazed around the room. It was a strange mixture of dates and places. The half-panelled walls may well have belonged to the original farmer of the seventeenth century. They were ornamented on the lower part by a line of modern watercolours. Above, where the yellow plaster took the place of the oak, a fine collection of South American utensils and

weapons was hung. I assumed that they had been hung there by either Ferguson himself or his wife as a reminder of that faraway country from which they had come.

Holmes rose, with that quick curiosity of an eager mind, and examined the items with care. He returned with his eyes full of thought.

'Hello,' he said to something in the corner.

A spaniel had lain in a basket at the edge of the room. It came slowly forward towards its master, walking with difficulty. Its hind legs moved irregularly and its tail was on the ground. It licked Ferguson's hand.

'What is it, Mr Holmes?' said Ferguson, aware of Holmes' gaze.

'The dog. What's the matter with it?'

'That's what puzzled the vet. A sort of paralysis. Spinal meningitis, he thought. But it is passing, thankfully. He'll be all right soon – won't you, Carlo?'

A shiver of agreement passed through the drooping tail. The

dog's mournful eyes passed from one of us to the other. He knew that we were talking about him.

'Did it come on suddenly?'

I wondered at Holmes' interest in the animal. He had never shown any particular liking for dogs before.

'In a single night.'

'How long ago?'

'It may have been four months ago.'

'Very remarkable.'

'What do you see in it,
Mr Holmes?' I could see
Ferguson's rising irritation
as he looked from the dog
to Holmes. He gripped the
arms of his chair and leaned
forward, a little breathlessly.

'A confirmation of what I had
already thought.'

Ferguson practically shot out
of his chair in frustration. 'For
heaven's sake, what do you see,
Mr Holmes? It may be merely
a puzzle to you, but it is life and

death to me! My wife a would-be murderer – my child in constant danger! Don't play with me, Mr Holmes. It is too terribly serious.'

The man who had once been

a rugby three-quarter was trembling all over.

Holmes put a soothing hand on his arm and gently pulled

him back into the chair. 'I
fear that there is pain for you,
Mr Ferguson, whatever the
solution may be,' he said. 'I
wish to spare you all I can.
I cannot say more for the
moment, but before I leave
this house I hope I may have
something definite.'

'Please God that you may! If
you will excuse me, gentlemen,
I will go up to my wife's room
and see if there has been any
change in her condition.'

He was away some minutes, during which Holmes resumed his examination of the curiosities on the wall. When our host returned it was clear from his downcast face that he had made no progress. He brought with him a tall, slim Hispanic girl.

'The tea is ready, Dolores,' said Ferguson. 'See that

your mistress has everything she needs.'

'She very ill,' cried the girl, looking with indignant eyes at her employer. 'She no ask for food. She very ill. She need doctor. I frightened to stay alone with her without doctor.'

Ferguson looked at me with a question in his eyes.

I smiled. 'I should be glad to be of use,' I said.

'Would your mistress see

Doctor Watson?' Ferguson asked the girl.

'I take him. I no ask. She need doctor.'

I stood and nodded at Dolores. 'Then I'll come with you at once.'

I followed the girl, who was quivering with strong emotion, up the stairs and along an ancient corridor. At the end was a massive door with an iron handle and lock. I thought, as I looked at it, that Ferguson would find it very difficult to force his way to see his wife if she did not wish it.

The girl took a key from her pocket, inserted it in the lock, and turned. The heavy oak planks creaked on their old hinges as she opened the door.

I went in and she swiftly followed, closing and locking the door behind her.

On the bed lay a woman who clearly had a high fever. She was only half conscious, but as I entered she raised a pair of frightened but beautiful eyes and glared at me in apprehension. Seeing a stranger, she appeared to be relieved and sank back with a sigh onto the pillow.

I stepped up to her. 'I'm a doctor,' I said, trying to reassure her. She lay still as I took her pulse and felt her brow. It was hot and her pulse was racing, yet my impression was that the condition was due to mental and nervous excitement rather than an actual seizure.

'She lie like that one day, two day. I 'fraid she die,' said the girl.

The woman turned her flushed and handsome face towards me. 'Where is my husband?'

'He is downstairs and wishes
to see you.'

'I will not see him.' Then
she seemed to wander off into
delirium. 'A fiend! A fiend! Oh,
what shall I do with this devil?'

'Can I help you in any way?'

'No. No one can help. It
is finished. All is destroyed.
Whatever I do, all is destroyed.'

The woman must have
some strange delusion. I could
not believe that honest Bob
Ferguson could possibly be seen

as a fiend or devil. I was the only one with access to the lady, so the task of discovering the source of this delusion fell to me. I resolved to discover more.

'Madam,' I said, 'your husband loves you dearly. He is deeply grieved at this happening.'

Again she turned those glorious eyes on me.

'He loves me. Yes. But do I not love him? Do I not love him so much that I would sacrifice myself rather than break his dear heart? That is how I love him. And yet he thinks I could do something so horrible! That he could speak to me like that!'

'He is full of grief, but he cannot understand.'

'No, he cannot understand, but he should trust.'

'Won't you see him?' I coaxed.

'No, no, I cannot forget those terrible words nor the look on his face. I will not see him. Go now. You can do nothing for me. Tell him only one thing: I

want my child. I have the right
to my child. That is the only
message I can send him.' She
turned her face to the wall and
would say no more despite
my attempts to engage her in
further conversation.

I returned to the room
downstairs, where Ferguson
and Holmes still sat by the fire.
Ferguson listened moodily to
my account of the interview.

'How can I send her the child?'
he said. 'How do I know what

strange impulse might come upon her? How can I ever forget how she rose from beside him with his blood on her lips?' He shuddered at the memory. 'The child is safe with Mrs Mason, and there he must remain.'

A smartly dressed maid had brought in some tea. As she was serving it, the door opened and a youth entered the room. He was a remarkable lad, pale-faced and fair-haired, with excitable pale-blue eyes that blazed into a sudden flame of emotion and joy as he saw his father. He rushed forward and threw his arms round his neck as if he had not seen his father in years.

'Oh, Daddy!' he cried. 'I did not know that you were due to return home yet. I should have been here to meet you. Oh, I am so glad to see you!'

Ferguson gently disengaged himself from the embrace, looking a little embarrassed.

'Dear old chap,' he said, patting the flaxen head with a very tender hand. 'I came early because my friends, Mr Holmes and Doctor Watson, have been persuaded to come down and spend an evening with us.'

'Is that Mr Holmes, the detective?'

'Yes.'

The youth looked at us with a

very penetrating and, it seemed to me, unfriendly gaze.

'What about your other child, Mr Ferguson?' asked Holmes. 'Might we meet the baby?'

'Jacky, ask Mrs Mason to bring the baby down,' said Ferguson.

The boy went off with a shambling gait that told my medical eyes that he was suffering from a weak spine.

Soon he returned, and behind him came a tall, gaunt woman

carrying a child in her arms.
A very beautiful child, with
golden hair and dark eyes: a
wonderful mixture of the Saxon
father and Latin mother.

Ferguson was evidently
devoted to him, for he took him
into his arms and
fondled him most
tenderly.

'Fancy anyone
having the heart
to hurt him,' he
muttered as he

glanced down at the child.

It was at this moment that I chanced to glance at Holmes, and saw a strange intensity in his expression. His face was as if it had been carved out of old ivory, and his eyes, which

had glanced for a moment at father and child, were now fixed with eager curiosity upon something at the other side of the room. Following his gaze, I could only guess that he was looking out through the window at the melancholy, dripping garden, but I had no idea what could be so interesting. A shutter had half closed outside and obstructed the view, but nevertheless it was certainly at the window that Holmes was fixing his concentrated attention.

Then he smiled, and his eyes
came back to the baby. On
its chubby neck there was a
small puckered mark. Without
speaking, Holmes examined
it with care. Finally, he shook
one of the dimpled fists
that waved in front
of him.

'Goodbye, little man. You have had a strange start in life. Nurse, I would like to have a word with you in private.'

He took her aside and spoke earnestly for a few minutes. I only heard the last words: 'Your anxiety, I hope, will soon be set to rest.'

The woman, who seemed to be a sour, silent kind of person, took a breath and nodded gratefully at Holmes before leaving with the child.

'What is Mrs Mason like?' asked Holmes.

Ferguson looked puzzled at the question but answered Holmes dutifully. 'Despite her rather unfriendly appearance, she has a heart of gold and she is devoted to the child.'

'Do you like her, Jack?'

Holmes turned suddenly to the boy.

Jack's expressive face clouded over, and he shook his head.

'Jacky has very strong likes and dislikes,' said Ferguson, putting his arm around the boy. 'Luckily, I am one of his likes.' The boy cooed and nestled his head upon his father's chest.

Ferguson gently removed him.
'Run away, little Jacky,' he said,
and watched his son with loving
eyes until he disappeared. 'Now,
Mr Holmes,' he continued,
when the boy was gone. 'I really
feel that I have brought you
here on a fool's errand, for what
can you possibly do but offer
your sympathy? It must be a
very delicate and complex affair
from your point of view.'

'It is certainly delicate,' said
my friend, with an amused

smile, 'but I'm not sure as to
its complexity. Each point has
been confirmed by a number
of unrelated incidents, and I
can confidently say that we
have reached our goal. I had,
in fact, reached it before we
left Baker Street. The rest has
merely been observation and
confirmation.'

Ferguson put a hand on his
furrowed forehead. 'For heaven's
sake, Holmes,' he said hoarsely,
'if you can see the truth in

this matter, do not keep me in suspense. How do I stand? What shall I do? I don't care how you found your facts so long as you have really got them.'

I understood Ferguson's frustration; Holmes' fondness for drama sometimes got in the way of helping his clients. Privately I thought Ferguson was doing an admirable job of remaining calm in what must be a frightening situation.

Holmes smiled graciously and

I hoped that he may have recognised just how distressing this case must be for Ferguson. 'Certainly I owe you an explanation, and you shall have it. But will you permit me to handle the matter in my own way? Is the lady well enough to see us, Watson?'

'She is ill, but she is quite rational.'

'Very good. It is only in her presence that we can clear the matter up. Let us go up to her.'

'She will not see me,' cried

Ferguson.

'Oh, yes, she will,' said
Holmes. He scribbled a few
lines on a sheet of paper. 'You
go first, Watson, and have the
goodness to give the lady this
note.'

I went

upstairs again and knocked gently on the locked door. Dolores opened it cautiously and I handed her the note. A minute later I heard a cry from within; a cry in which joy and surprise seemed to be blended. Dolores looked out.

'She will see them. She will listen,' she said.

At my call, Ferguson and Holmes came up. As we entered the room, Ferguson took a step or two towards his wife, who was now sitting up in bed, but she held out her hand to hold him back. He sank into an armchair instead. Holmes sat down beside him after bowing to the lady, who looked at him with wide-eyed amazement.

'Dolores does not need to be here,' said Holmes, but seeing the look on the lady's face, he added, 'Oh, very well, madam, if you would rather she stayed I see no objection. Now, Mr Ferguson, I am a busy man with many calls, and my methods have to be short and direct. The swiftest surgery is the least painful. Let me first say what will ease your mind. Your wife is a very good, a very loving, and a very mistreated woman.'

Ferguson sat up with a cry of joy. 'Prove that, Mr Holmes, and I am in your debt forever.'

'I will do so, but in doing so I must wound you deeply.'

'I care nothing so long as you clear my wife. Everything on earth is insignificant compared to that.'

'Let me tell you then, the train of reasoning that passed through my mind in Baker Street. The idea of a vampire was to me absurd. Such things do not happen. And yet your observation was precise. You had seen the lady rise from beside the child's cot with blood upon her lips.'

'I did.'

'Did it not occur to you that a bleeding wound may be sucked for some other purpose than to draw the blood from it?

Was there not a queen in English history who sucked such a wound to draw poison from it?'

'Poison!'

'This is a South American household. My instinct felt the presence of those weapons on the wall before my eyes ever saw them. It might have been

Eleanor of Castile
Queen of England (1241-1290) and wife of Edward I. Believed to have sucked poison from a dagger wound in her husband's arm, saving the king's life.

some other poison, but that
was what occurred to me. When
I saw that little empty quiver
beside the small bird-bow, it was
just what I expected to see. If the
child were pricked with one of
those arrows dipped in curare,
or some other devilish drug, it

would mean death if the toxin were not sucked out quickly.'

Ferguson's expression was one of shock and gradual realisation. My heart sank as I knew what was coming next.

'And the dog!' went on Holmes. 'If one were to use such poison, would one not try it out first in order to see that it had not lost its power? I did not foresee the dog, but at least I understood him and he fitted into my reconstruction of events.

101

'Now do you understand?'
Holmes said gently. 'Your wife
feared such an attack. She saw
it happen and saved the child's
life, and yet she shied away from
telling you the truth, for she
knew how you loved the boy
and feared that
it would break
your heart.'
    'Jacky!'
    'I watched
him just now.

His face was clearly reflected
in the glass of the window
where the shutter formed
a background. I saw such
jealousy, such cruel hatred,
as I have seldom seen on a
human face.'

'My Jacky!'

'You have to face it, Mr Ferguson. It is more painful because it is a distorted love; a maniacal, exaggerated love for you, and possibly for his dead mother, which has prompted his action. His very soul is consumed with jealousy and hatred for this splendid child of your second wife.'

'Good God! It is incredible!'

'Have I spoken the truth, madam?'

The lady was sobbing,
with her face buried in the
pillows. Now she turned to her
husband.

'How could I tell you, Bob?
I felt the blow it would be to
you. It was better that I should
wait, and that it should come
from some other lips than mine.

105

When the gentleman, who seems to have powers of magic, wrote that he knew everything, I was glad.'

'I think a year at sea would be my suggestion for Master Jacky,' said Holmes, rising from his chair. 'Only one thing is still unclear, madam. We can quite understand your attacks upon Master Jacky. There is a limit to a mother's patience. But how did you dare to leave the child these last two days that you have been in this room?'

'I had told Mrs Mason the truth. She knew the danger.'

'Exactly. So I imagined.'

Ferguson was standing by the bed, his hands quivering and his eyes brimming with tears.

'This, I fancy, is the time for our exit, Watson,' said Holmes in a whisper, ushering Dolores in front of us. 'I think we may leave them to settle the rest among themselves.'

As we passed the bed, a small piece of paper fluttered to the floor. I could just make out the few words on it.

My dear madam,
I know all. Your misery will soon be over.
                    Yours respectfully,
                    Sherlock Holmes

We left the room and closed the door behind us.

The next day, Holmes replied to the original letter he had received from Ferguson's solicitors.

Baker Street,
November 21st

Re: Vampires

Sir - Referring to your letter of the 19th,
I am writing to inform you that I have
looked into the enquiry of your client,
Mr Robert Ferguson, of Ferguson and
Muirhead, tea brokers, of Mincing Lane,
and the matter has been brought to a
satisfactory conclusion.
With thanks for your recommendation,

I am, sir, faithfully yours,

Sherlock Holmes